For my family—George, Holly, Derek, and George C.

I would like to thank my agent, Amy Berkower, and my editor, Megan Tingley, for their unflagging support, enthusiasm, and patience. It's been a joy to work with designer Stephen Blauweiss and photographer Ogden Gigli, who brought skill, artistry, and good humor to this challenging project. My thanks also go to Amy Lowenhar for pitching in when needed to help find the stamps.

Little, Brown and Company

Hachette Book Group USA
237 Park Avenue, New York, NY 10169
Visit our Web site at www.lb-kids.com

First Edition: September 2007

ISBN-13: 978-0-316-81172-9
ISBN-10: 0-316-81172-6

10 9 8 7 6 5 4 3 2 1

WORZ

Printed in the U.S.A.

Photo of Joan Steiner by Michael Fredericks
Thomas Lindley: taxi, ocean liner, and airplane

Magnifying glass—Scott Rothstein/Shutterstock

Stamps
Shutterstock: 2.) Viking helmet—Johanna Goodyear; 19.) African mask—Slobodan Djajic; 26.) Polynesian Dancer—K. Thorsen; 27.) Sydney Harbor—Martin Preston; 34.) Tepees—Matt Ragen; 35.) Indian chief—John Kirinic; 39.) Hudson Valley

istock: 1.) Holland windmill; 3.) Big Ben—Deejpilot; 4.) Loch Ness; 5.) cathedral window; 11.) Pisa—Helen Shorey; 17.) South African Kudu; 20.) Taj mahal; 30.) Machu Picchu; 36.) Egret

Stephen Blauweiss: 9.) Paris bridge; 10.) Burg Stahleck; 12.) Venice; 15.) Greece; 23.) Mount Fuji; 31.) Chrysler building

Wikipedia: 13.) Spain—Daniel Csorfoly a.k.a. Dubaduba; 14.) Tchaikovsky, 1874; 37.) Marlin

Big Stock Photo: 22.) Japanese Garden; 24.) Great Wall of China; 29.) Antarctica

Keith Pettinato: 6.) York Minster; 28.) Easter Island

Various: 6.); 7.) Chateau Palmer — Indexstock, MedioImages, Inc.; 8.)Arc de Triomphe—Daniel Lentz/istock; 12.) Venice — Freefoto, Ian Britton; 16) Pyramid-inframe/stockxpert; 18.) African Village—Fotolia; 21.) Thai dancer—roren/stockxpert; 25.) Hong Kong—Richard Caraballo; 32.) Golden Gate Bridge—cphoto 33.) Florida—U.S. Map Registry; 38.) Cape Cod—NASA

LOOK-ALIKES®
∞ Around the World ∞

Concept, Constructions & Text by
JOAN STEINER

Design by Stephen Blauweiss   Photography by Ogden Gigli

Megan Tingley Books
LITTLE, BROWN AND COMPANY
New York ∞ Boston

WELCOME TO THE WORLD OF LOOK-ALIKES!

No ordinary postcard would show you that the turrets of a French chateau look just like ice cream cones! That's just one of hundreds of amazing things you'll discover in this album. Come along on a look-alikes trip around the world and be astonished by what you find!

ORDINARY POSTCARD

LOOK-ALIKES POSTCARD

At the end of the album, you'll find more about each of the places we visited and a list of all the look-alikes in each postcard.

But don't peek till you're done searching.
The more you look, the more you see!

SO OFF WE GO! STARTING IN EUROPE...
Holland was all in bloom.

In Scandinavia, we learned
about the Vikings.

England was rich in tradition,
and Scotland rich in mystery.

Britannia Rules

Nessie!

RAM'S HEAD
PUB

52
Look-Alikes

We saw lots of cathedrals

York Minster Cathedral, York, England

and great houses called chateaux.

Loire Valley

90
Look-Alikes

But in the end, coming home is always sweet!

Greetings from Claverack, New York

CAPE COD

Provincetown
Truro
Wellfleet
Eastham
Orleans
Dennis
Brewster
Barnstable
Yarmouth

N
W E
S

Morro Bay, California

Red's Lobster Shack

38 Look-Alikes

SOUTH PADRE ISLAND, TEXAS

GONE FISHIN'!

... to the Rockies and Great Plains stretching north.

MANITOBA

Greetings from
Big Chief,
South
Dakota

37
Look-Alikes

DEVIL'S TOWER
WYOMING

NEW YORK

HI! FROM SAN FRANCISCO

Bienvenidos!
PERU

A. Muñoz
Pre-Columbian
Antiquities

3 Calle del
Mundo

Quito,
Ecuador

29
Look-Alikes

And we sailed to some of the remotest places on earth...

to marvel at prehistoric statues

"Son, one day all this will be yours."

and to fall in love with penguins

POLYNESIAN PARADISE

We went from tropical beaches

to exciting cities.

A "Shoevenir" of New Guinea

28
Look-Alikes

萬里長城

PEKING DUCK

北京烤鴨

FRIED NOODLES

In China, land of contrasts, the oldest of the old meets the newest of the new.

40
Look-Alikes

We saw a graceful Thai dancer

Visit Thailand!

38 Look-Alikes

and visited a serene Japanese garden.

INDIA

A Traditional Nigerian Village

49 Look-Alikes

Off the beaten track, we learned about the way of life in traditional villages.

CEREMONIAL MASKS

Man fears time, yet time fears the Pyramids.
— Arab proverb

THEN ON TO AFRICA...

We couldn't wait to see the pyramids

and the game parks full of animals.

KUDU • SOUTH AFRICA

We island-hopped in Greece.

Temple ruins, Delos, Greece

OLIVE OIL

Product of Greece

29 Look-Alikes

Everywhere we went, there was dancing.

Olé!

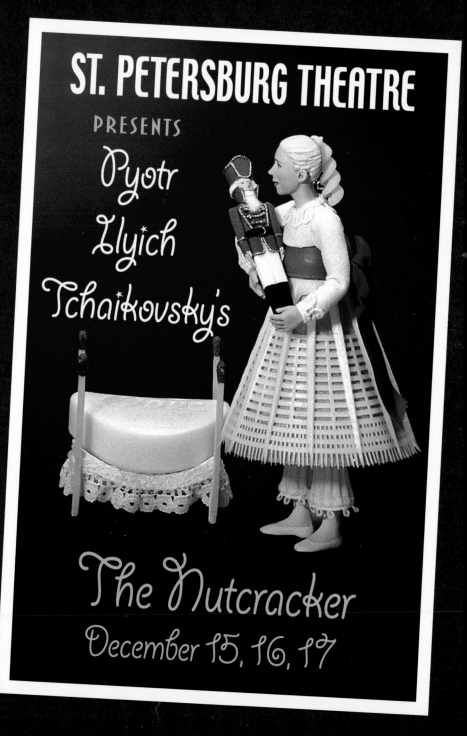

ST. PETERSBURG THEATRE

PRESENTS

Pyotr
Ilyich
Tchaikovsky's

The Nutcracker
December 15, 16, 17

The food in Italy was just amazing!

"CIAO" FROM ITALY

LA BELLA VENEZIA

49
Look-Alikes

Greetings from Germany's beautiful Rhine Valley

Düsseldorf Delicatessen

"OUR WURST IS BEST!"

Arc de Triomphe as seen from Tuileries Gardens

Everyone should visit Paris in the spring!

Paris
City of Art

Windmills are not only a symbol of Holland; they actually helped to create the country by pumping away the water that once covered much of the low-lying land—land that now makes Holland the tulip capital of the world.

THE LOOK-ALIKES: Metronome, combs, chopsticks, broccoli, wooden matches, corn kernels, jelly beans, pistachios (natural and red), fake fingernails, and green beans.

Scandinavia is a region that includes the countries of Norway, Sweden, and Denmark. The ancestors of today's peace-loving Scandinavians were fierce sea rovers and warriors known as the Vikings.

THE LOOK-ALIKES: Bottom half of tea ball, cashew nuts, kiwi fruit*, gloves, snap, ballpoint pen, lid for coffee container, spiral notepad, paintbrush, and arrow.
*hard to see

From its corner at the Houses of Parliament, Big Ben's familiar clock chimes ring out over the city of London. The city's famous double-decker red buses are perfect for sightseeing.

THE LOOK-ALIKES: Carpenter's folding rulers, clothespins, compass, wishbones, Eiffel Tower souvenir, pencils, lace, toy train track, pearls, snaps*, waffles, harmonicas, white marble, and crown-shaped hinge.

*hard to see

4. Nessie

Thousands of people visit beautiful Loch Ness every year hoping to catch a glimpse of its legendary monster, affectionately known as Nessie. So far, no one has been able to prove that she exists, though many "sightings" have been reported.

THE LOOK-ALIKES: Coat hook, wooden flute, meat tenderizer mallets, spiral pad paper (torn off), coin wrappers, small paper bag, comb, broccoli, plaid jacket, and long-haired sheep fur.

5. Cathedral Window

Medieval cathedrals are famous for their magnificent stained glass windows. In the Middle Ages, when few people could read, the people could see the stories of the Bible and of history "written" in the sparkling colored light of cathedral windows.

THE LOOK-ALIKES: Butterflies, embroidery hoop, man-shaped paper clip, small hair grip, whistles, needle-nose pliers, keys, shamrock stickers, jacks, mechanical pencils, playing cards, rope, clothespins, recorders (tops only), chess pieces, lace, and dog biscuits*.

*hard to see

6. York Minster

York's magnificent cathedral, or "minster," was completed in 1470 and is the largest medieval church in Northern Europe. The church has been used as a place of worship for nearly 1,000 years!

THE LOOK-ALIKES: Cocktail forks, chess bishops, matches, wooden block, rusty saw blade, box of matches, tiny pen, pencil-tip eraser, and rubber stamp.

7. Chateau

Many of the grand houses of Europe and their formal gardens are open to visitors. The Loire Valley of France is famous for its chateaux, with more than 300.

THE LOOK-ALIKES: Ice cream cones, golf tee, baby bottle nipple, overalls buckles, toilet paper rolls, spools of thread, garter hook, green knitted socks*, bell, (artificial) artichoke*, green glove, champagne cork cage, wooden block, pom-pom upholstery trim, doormat, thimbles, nonpareils candy, blue CD, saltshaker, and cotton (clouds).

*hard to see

8. Arc de Triomphe

Standing at the place in Paris where 12 avenues come together, the Arc de Triomphe is so colossal that a daredevil pilot once flew his plane through it.

THE LOOK-ALIKES: Zipper and zipper pulls, bookends, dice, bell, gum erasers, circuit board, overalls buckle, marble, old-fashioned safety razor, saltshaker tops, candlestick, cheese box, pen nibs, pencils, tiny earrings, fancy soap, maple seeds, vending machine "bubble" with toy ring inside, hose nozzle, champagne cork cages, tortilla chip, toothpick, Christmas lightbulb, juicer, and almonds.

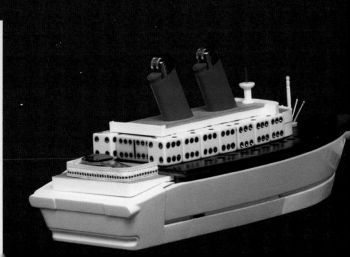

Paris is not only a city of art but a city of artists. Her 37 bridges are favorite places for painters to set up their easels, seeking inspiration from the beauty of the city and the river Seine.

THE LOOK-ALIKES: Scissors, rubber stamp*, matchbooks, coat hooks, wooden hanger, corn kernels, parsley, opera glasses, brass hose nozzle, coin purses, stamps, champagne cork cages, chess castle, button, wooden matches and matchbox, wishbone, and playing cards.
*hard to see

Famed for its stunning natural beauty, its castles, cathedrals, and vineyards, the Rhine Valley is also a source of myth and legend. According to German folklore, a Rhine maiden named Lorelei could lure sailors with the beauty of her singing to wreck their ships on the rocks of the shore.

THE LOOK-ALIKES: Crayon, food grater, bell, wooden block, corduroy, wrench, harmonica, bread, funnel, miniature beer steins, cell phone, dollhouse furniture, fuzzy green rabbit, and flip-flops.

The Leaning Tower of Pisa is one of the most famous symbols of Italy. The bell tower of the cathedral started to lean soon after construction began in 1173 . . . but the Pisans kept building it anyway!

THE LOOK-ALIKES: Cookies (two kinds), insulated staples, acorns, rubber stamps, leaves, sea horse, chess castle, and cheesy cracker.

2. Venice

The beautiful medieval city of Venice is built on hundreds of tiny islands in a lagoon. Where other cities have streets, Venice has its famous canals. And where other people take cars or buses, Venetians take boats.

THE LOOK-ALIKES: Nutcracker, pasta ribbons, buttons, wishbones, sugar packet, cheesy crackers, birthday candles, wooden matches, ravioli, Chinese paintbrushes, cocktail forks, chess castles, chocolate bar, comb, rotten bananas, pencils, clothespins, peppermint candy sticks, chess pawns, cinnamon sticks, and glass cutter.

13. Spain

Flamenco is a merging of three arts—song, dance, and music—which first took recognizable form among *gitanos* (Gypsies) in southern Spain. Here, a flamenco dancer weaves her spell in the 600-year-old courtyard of Seville's splendid royal residence, the Real Alcázar.

THE LOOK-ALIKES: Breakfast cereal, elbow macaroni, honey dippers, playing cards, castanet, Valentine candy, zippers, and silk cornflowers.

4. Nutcracker

Russia is the great home of classical ballet. The beloved *Nutcracker*, set to music by the brilliant Russian composer Tchaikovsky, is performed all around the world every Christmas season to the delight of children and adults alike.

THE LOOK-ALIKES: Shuttlecock, pasta twist, travel-size soap, and matchsticks.

15. Greek Islands

Over 2,000 years ago, in what is called the Golden Age of Greece, there was a great flowering of ideas and arts that still shapes our world and our thinking today. Temple ruins remind us of this glorious time that laid the foundation for Western civilization.

THE LOOK-ALIKES: Pasta tubes, dog biscuits, wooden blocks, wooden flute, fake fur, natural pistachios, natural sponge, dice, tiny bell, toy baby bottle, white spiral shell, Legos®, pop-up bottle top, tiny earring, acorn cap, and votive candle.

16. Pyramids

The Great Pyramid at Giza is considered the most massive building ever erected in the entire world, which is particularly remarkable when we remember that it was constructed 4,500 years ago!

THE LOOK-ALIKES: Leg of brown baby doll, crab shell, fig bar, white spiral seashell, matzo, alphabet block, paintbrushes, feathers, green tassels, cinnamon sticks, bone, piece of firewood*, and brown rice.
*hard to see

17. South Africa

South Africa's Kruger National Park, one of the world's foremost game sanctuaries, provides safe refuge for nearly 850 species of animals, including this stately kudu antelope with his corkscrew horns.

THE LOOK-ALIKES: Old-fashioned hairpin, pistachio shells, almond, birch bark, feathers, rope, and stuffed animal.

18. African Village

Many Africans still follow a tribal way of life by living in mud-hut villages with their extended families, keeping their own animals, and tending the land.

THE LOOK-ALIKES: Tassels, pretzel sticks, muffin, magnets, rice cakes, hot-beverage sleeve, basket,* wooden block, acorns, tiny (artificial) bird's nest, sprigs of thyme, jelly beans, walnut shell, ponytail elastic, and (artificial) butterfly wings.
*hard to see

19. African Masks

Masks are an essential part of African tribal ceremonies and rituals. Tribesmen and women use masks to make contact with the world of powerful unseen spirits and to ask for their blessing and protection.

THE LOOK-ALIKES:
CAT: Rusty pulley, licorice twists, pony tail elastic, green Life Savers, red balloon*, fuzzy leopard print slippers, wishbone, and paper candy cup.
ANTELOPE: Gloves, salted sunflower seeds, photo corner, guitar pick, black-eyed peas, and Chinese fried noodles.

20. Taj Mahal

Considered by many to be the most beautiful building in the world, the Taj Mahal was built by a grief-stricken 17th-century Indian ruler as a burial place for his favorite wife. More than 20,000 laborers worked every day for 11 years to complete this monument to love.

THE LOOK-ALIKES: Onions, ballet slipper and small white shoes, price tags, straws, pushpins, lace, recorders, white chocolate bars, Brussels sprouts, rosemary, photo corners, and jingle bells.

21. Thai Dancer

Thai dance, known as "Fawn Thai," is the main dramatic art form of Thailand. Originally performed for the royal courts of old Siam, performances in olden times could sometimes last an entire day! The spire-shaped headdress is traditional.

THE LOOK-ALIKES: Spark plugs, gold candy cup, two-ended wrench, spoon, horseshoe crab shell, combs, snakeskin, old food grater, bell, paper coffee cup with sleeve, parsley, cookies, and backgammon board.

22. Japanese Garden

Not just a pretty place, the Japanese garden is intended to be a spiritual haven that evokes feelings of peace and harmony and that encourages contemplation. Every element in a Japanese garden has meaning and was included for a reason.

THE LOOK-ALIKES: Blue birthday candle holder, silk flower, pretzels, breadsticks, green fuzzy yarn, dark green tassels, Brazil nuts, velvet brocade fabric, rock candy, crumpled plastic wrap, safety pins, and ball-headed pin.

23. Mount Fuji

The nearly perfect cone of Mount Fuji is a favorite subject of Japanese artists and a very popular summer destination for climbers. Some hikers climb all through the night so as to make it to the summit by the next morning for the sunrise!

THE LOOK-ALIKES: Leg in woolly stocking, doily, green beans, tassels, tissue box in straw holder, white coral, and popcorn.

24. Great Wall of China

The Great Wall of China, parts of which date back more than 2,000 years, is the largest building project every carried out by humans. The watchtowers served both to guard the wall and to communicate with the capital by sending signals—smoke by day, fire by night. 萬里長城 is "Great Wall of China" in Chinese.

THE LOOK-ALIKES: Zippers and zipper pulls, electrical plugs, throw pillows, photo corners, rusty old hinge, old Chinese coin, wishbones, and parsley.

25. Hong Kong

In the shadow of glittering skyscrapers, an ancient Chinese boat called a junk plies the water of Hong Kong harbor.

THE LOOK-ALIKES: Coffee filters (folded), chopsticks, cashews, small Chinese soap in wrapper, restaurant guest check, carpenter's folding ruler, Mah Jongg tiles, sugar cubes, telephone handset, wooden soap dish, matchboxes, ice cube tray, sandwich cookies, pill organizer box, and comb.

26. Polynesia

In Polynesia, a grass-skirted dancer tells stories with her hands. When she holds her hands in a horizontal position and gently ripples her fingers, it means "across the water."

THE LOOK-ALIKES: Tassel, ponytail elastic, baby tooth, breadcrumbs, cocoa-covered candy balls, dried figs, and feathers.

27. Sydney Opera House

The Sydney Opera House is one of the most distinctive buildings of the 20th century. Overlooking Sydney Harbor, its unique roof suggests a ship at full sail. In the less than 40 years of its existence, the Opera House has become the most recognized symbol of Australia.

THE LOOK-ALIKES: Pistachios, garlic clove, clothespin, hair clips, and tiny dice.

28. Easter Island

Over 2,000 miles from the nearest settlement, Easter Island is one of the loneliest islands in the world. Now a national park of Chile, it is famous for its huge stone figures known as *moai*. No living person knows why they were carved.

THE LOOK-ALIKES: Foot with sock, doorstop, acorn cap, caramels, and Brazil nuts.

29. Antarctica

There are many different kinds of penguins and, contrary to what some might think, they do not all live in icy places. But all the penguins in the world do live in the southern hemisphere. You'll never find one at the North Pole!

THE LOOK-ALIKES: Salted sunflower seed, egg, wishbone, mouse cat toy, lentils, lace, and Styrofoam packing material.

30. Machu Picchu

Sometimes called the Lost City of the Incas, Machu Picchu is a well-preserved ruin from before the time of Columbus, located high up on a ridge in the Andes Mountains. How the Incas moved and placed the enormous blocks of stone they used to build the city is a mystery to this day.

THE LOOK-ALIKES: Sliced bread, peanut butter, egg cartons, and throw pillows. (Grass is made with green powder—not a look-alike.)

INSET: Hacky sack, candy fruit slice, birthday candle, ribbed pasta tubes, napkin, and back of jigsaw puzzle.

31. Chrysler Building

Completed in 1930, the elegant Chrysler Building is still one of the most distinctive features of the Manhattan skyline. Built as the headquarters of the Chrysler automobile company, it is decorated with replicas of hood ornaments and radiator caps!

THE LOOK-ALIKES: Awl, hair clips, tennis racket, window latches, tray, pennies, and toy train tracks*.
*hard to see

32. Golden Gate Bridge

The "Golden Gate" is the opening from the Pacific Ocean into the San Francisco Bay. Before the bridge was built, people had to make this crossing by boat or go a very long way around the bay.

THE LOOK-ALIKES: Carpenter's level, red paper clips, pushpins, posable mannequins, red toy pliers, moth, green barrette, and clams.

33. Florida

Called the Sunshine State because of its wonderful climate, Florida offers so much for vacationers: beautiful beaches, boating, fishing, amusement parks, heritage sites, golf, spas, outdoor adventures, and nature preserves—plus delicious orange juice!

THE LOOK-ALIKES, CLOCKWISE FROM TOP: Maple seeds, straw hat, thumbtack, supermarket saving stamp, green tassels, brown rice*, chain, candy corn, button, ballpoint pen, cotton balls, guitar pick, wooden match, barrette, party horns, tiny trumpet and drum Christmas ornaments, crayon tips, kazoo, coin purse, flashlights, opera glasses, and fancy giftwrap bow.
*hard to see

34. Tepees

For the Plains Indians, tepees were movable homes, much like tents, that enabled them to follow the herds of buffalo that supplied them with food and hides.

THE LOOK-ALIKES: Seashells, lentils, okra, cowhide, and folding knives.

35. Indian Chief

The feathers in an Indian's warbonnet had to be earned through deeds of bravery in battle. Every feather told a story of some courageous act. The eagle was considered by the Indian as the greatest and most powerful of all birds, so the finest bonnets were made out of its feathers.

THE LOOK-ALIKES: Makeup applicators, snap, safety pin, paper coin wrapper, ponytail elastic, photo corners, pickup stick, and sprouted potatoes.

36. Egret

All of Morro Bay is a bird sanctuary and nature preserve. It provides an excellent habitat for this great egret, an elegant white bird that stalks its prey slowly and methodically in shallow water.

THE LOOK-ALIKES: Ladle, gloves, Chinese paintbrushes, Styrofoam cup, and ink bottle.

37. Marlin

Charter a boat with your buddies and head out for the Gulf's deep water! The most prized trophy is the blue marlin, which can exceed 400 pounds. Most fisherman are just in it for the thrill of the hunt, so they release the giant fish that they catch.

THE LOOK-ALIKES: Feather, tiny doily, and Legos®.

38. Cape Cod

Thanks to the foresight of President John F. Kennedy, 40 miles of Cape Cod's pristine beaches and dunes were declared a National Seashore, thereby protecting them from development forever.

THE LOOK-ALIKES—MAP: Arm in sleeve and glove, plastic number 35, pen nibs, bottle cap, shark's tooth; LAUGHING GULL: Hand-shaped soap, balloon, chocolate truffle, black-eyed pea, piece of firewood; WHALE: Balloon, pancakes, chess castle, pushpin; LIGHTHOUSES: Tube of paint, die, pop-up bottle top, supermarket saving stamp, potatoes, pecans in shell, feathers; WINDMILL: Funnel, cocktail picks, hot beverage cup, plastic tag for bread bag, stick of gum*, pretzel sticks, towel, and parsley. *hard to see

39. Home

Claverack is a small rural community nestled in New York State's beautiful Hudson Valley. It is also Joan Steiner's hometown.

THE LOOK-ALIKES: Cake, kidney beans, crackers, jam-filled cookies, biscuits, cough drops, plastic candy box tray, silk rosebuds, Cheerios, wooden forks, paper fastener, dried figs, Valentine hearts (two sizes), Styrofoam packing "peanuts," tassels*, cotton, and cauliflower.
*hard to see

Bonus Look-Alikes

HOT AIR BALLOON: Lightbulb and parsley.
DUTCH GIRL CHEESE: Carry-out food container, souvenir wooden shoes, paper frill for drumsticks/chops, and embroidery hoop.
RAM'S HEAD PUB SIGN: Sponge, fossil spiral seashells, black-eyed peas, and clothing hook.
FRENCH FLAG: Knitting needle and tickets.
DELICATESSEN: Shelled peanuts*, hinge, garter hook, cut-off crayons and pastel sticks, pink pencil-tip eraser, and pebble.
OLIVE OIL: Balloon.
"INDIA": Dog biscuits.
TEMPLE TEA: Price tag, hair clips, abacus, and old Chinese coin*
PEKING DUCK: Football, pipe, hair clip, coyote fur, ball of crochet yarn, and spiral seashells.
NEW GUINEA "SHOEVENIR": Shoe, pink rubber ball, toothpicks, and tassel.
PRE-COLUMBIAN BIRD SCULPTURE: Cup, sweet potato, pecans, and red banana skin.
DEVIL'S TOWER: Muffin and bottle cap.
LOBSTER BIB: Red pistachios.
OCEAN LINER: Steam iron, dice, white domino, disposable lighters, key*, and white pushpin.
LOCOMOTIVE: Lamp socket, spool of thread, brass door bolt, buckle, ballpoint pen refill, safety pin, keys, and metal buttons.
AIRPLANE: Tube of paint, guitar pick, tiny nut (nuts-and-bolts type)*, and transparent button*.
TAXI: Black shoe, mushrooms, sewing needle, zipper slide, acorn, silver barrettes, and key chain clasp (door handle)*.

*hard to see

JOAN STEINER is a graduate of Barnard College and a self-taught artist. This is her fourth Look-Alikes book. Her previous books have sold more than one million copies and have been published in sixteen countries around the world. The recipient of numerous art and design awards, including a Society of Illustrators Award and a National Endowment for the Arts fellowship, Ms. Steiner lives in Claverack, New York.

I've enjoyed taking this trip around the world with you.

Happy travels!

Joan